COFFEE BREAK

AN EROTIC NOVELLA

BIG CITY ROMANCE
BOOK ONE

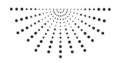

NAVY WINTERS

To the girl that wants to fuck on the first date...

Ride that dick, sis.

CONTENTS

TRIGGER WARNINGS AND SUCH...

PLEASE READ THIS SECTION

Seeing this means that you are about to read a book that may contain upsetting or triggering events. The listed events are general things you may encounter when you read a story of mine, not just this one in particular, so I urge you to read with caution and take care of yourself first and foremost.

This book may include:

- Other Woman/Man Drama
- Emotional/Physical Abuse
- Group/Adult/Kinky Activities
- Murder/Death
- Pineapple on Pizza

Reminder: My descriptions of kinky things do not represent any kink as a whole but my interpretation of and experience with it. ALWAYS do things that are SAFE, SANE, and CONSENSUAL. DO NOT use this literary work as an educational source or guide for any kink or kink-like activity.

OH AND ANOTHER THING.......

This is your reminder to charge your vibrator....

It's charged?

That's my dirty girl...

CHAPTER ONE

"Vanilla oat milk latte!"

Finally! It took them long enough to call out my order. I need the caffeine boost to get me through the therapy sessions I have to schedule today.

You'd think after 10 years working as a sex therapist nestled in the heart of Downtown Detroit that I would get a little excitement in my day. That isn't to say my job is boring or I don't like it. I love it but having to sit through a woman pouring out her feelings session after session only for her raggedy ass husband to look her in the face with confusion, as if he has never heard those words pour out of her face, makes me a bit cranky. Hence, needing my coffee fix before going into the office.

I stride across the room in my forest green slacks and white button-up that I paired with my favorite nude heels and matching peacoat. A pair of diamond and gold earrings rest in my ears completing my outfit. My waist-length box braids swing across the top of my plump ass and wide hips as I excused myself past the tired mom with three kids hanging off of her and the overworked college student talking to her friends a mile a minute before reaching the pickup station. I reach out to grab my cup when a hand with skin the color of cocoa shoots out and picks up my cup. Anger simmers beneath my skin because of the audacity of this hand to touch my lifeline of sanity!

Bringing my attention up the arm attached to the offending hand, I take in the man before me and what a man he is. My breath catches in my throat at the sight of the whitest teeth I have ever come across. He has to have at least a foot on my five-foot-two frame. His wide chest stretches his cream-colored scrubs almost to capacity while showing off the hard planes of his body. The man's biceps had to be as wide as one of my thighs, which is saying something when you have a body grown on collard greens and cornbread. Dragging my eyes upwards, I take in his well-groomed beard and mustache surrounding the softest lips I have ever seen. His brown eyes look at me with questions in them that I find myself wanting to answer.

The man I'm so obviously checking out clears his throat and I'm brought back to why I'm staring at him in the first place.

This asshole stole my coffee.

"That's mine. You picked up my drink." I say to him, raising my nose in the air.

"No. I'm pretty sure this one is mine." My pussy jumps from the deep, baritone timbre in his voice. I shake that off because I have to remember this man stole my cup of happiness when he saw me reaching for it.

"You ordered a vanilla oat milk latte?" I ask in disbelief.

He chuckles and his laugh is gorgeous. "A man can't order a latte?"

I fold my arms across my chest. "It's not the typical order for a man, no. I would expect more of a straight black coffee which, obviously, you've mistaken my drink for. So, if you'll be so kind as to turn my coffee loose, I'll take my drink and go now."

"Gorgeous, this is my order." He chuckles again and I wanna know what the hell is so funny. I want my drink so I can go. "How about this? We look at the label and see whose name is on it. If it's yours, I'll give you the cup and respectfully bow out."

"And if it's yours?" I inquire.

"If it's mine, you let me take you out to get a drink of your own."

Swallowing, I weigh them against each other. On the one hand, I get my damn drink and can conduct therapy sessions. On the other hand, I get to see more of this fine-ass man that God took his time with in every way.

"Okay. I'll take that bet. I'll be on my way as soon as you hand me MY coffee." I say.

He flashes that cute ass smile my way again before sliding the sleeve on the cup to display the label. He turns it in my direction before the name comes into view.

Fuck...

"I guess you owe me a date then, huh? My name is Choice by the way." He holds out his hand.

"I'm Tru," I say reluctantly, placing my hand in his to shake.

He holds on to my hand for a minute or two before releasing it and my body cries out for the warmth of his hand to return.

"Take my number, I'll pick up you tomorrow at 6. Dress warm."

After exchanging numbers, the barista sets my drink next to me. I slide the sleeve to verify the drink is mine before scooping it up and turning towards the door. I peek over my shoulder and Choice is still looking right at me. I hurry out the door and head towards the building where my office is located.

Lord be a fence because I'm sure to climb his ass before our date is over.

CHAPTER TWO

IT'S ALMOST a quarter to five when I step out of my hot shower. Grabbing my sandalwood and vanilla lotion along with my Vaseline, I sit at the foot of my bed before I moisturize myself from head to toe. The cold winters of the Midwest make it more than necessary for me to rub myself down in the protective ointment.

I slide on my black lace panties and the matching bra, checking out myself in my floor-length mirror propped against my bedroom wall.

Damn, I look good.

My phone chimes stealing my attention away from the mirror with an incoming video call from my best friend, Aeris. I've known her since the age of 4 since our moms were best friends. We are so inseparable that being in two different states doesn't hinder our relationship in the slightest. I do miss her but video and phone calls help.

I wipe off my hands on my discarded bath towel before answering it. "Hello, baby girl."

"Bitch, where you going shining like your momma slathered you down for the first day of school?"

"I'm going to mind my business! Something yo ass need to do!" I tease.

"Yeah, okay. Now when I pop up over there, I don't wanna hear a peep!" Aeris shouts.

"I'm going out with Choice, remember? I told you last night." I say as I finish moisturizing my leg.

"Oh! Right! You did tell me. Girl, my head be so gone these days. Do you know where you are going yet?"

"No, he told me to dress warm so I'm assuming it's going to be something outside or where it's cold." I grab my jeans from the bed and put them on.

"Outside?" Aeris says mimicking the Soulja Boy meme. "Homeboy don't know it's cold as fuck out there?"

I laugh hard because the same thought crossed my mind. Being born and raised in Detroit, you'd think after twenty-eight years here I would be used to the cold and snow. That would be an incorrect assumption as it seems every year gets colder and colder all the while my utter distaste for all that is ice and snow grows.

"I'm sure we'll go somewhere where it's warm, too. He still owes me my drink and I plan to collect."

"Mhmm... Well, you be on your best behavior and don't do nothing I wouldn't do!" She teases me before we say our goodbyes and I finish getting dressed.

Pulling on my navy blue sweater, I'm careful of my braids stacked on top of my head. I put them in a cute ponytail, and I'll be damned if I mess them up. I grab my black Ugg boots before spritzing my favorite perfume on my pressure points and head toward the front room.

Just as I finish pulling on my boots, my doorbell rings. I grab my necessities before pulling open the door to the finest black man that has ever darkened my doorstep.

Choice is dressed in all black, including the black Timberland boots on his feet. The black skullcap on his head hides the deep waves he sported yesterday.

"You ready to go or are you content on standing in the cold staring at me like I'm your next meal?" Choice's voice rumbles.

I roll my eyes and step outside before turning to lock the door. I can feel the heat radiating from Choice's body at my back. He hasn't moved an inch from where he stopped on my porch which has him invading my personal space. He grabs me around the waist and hugs me to his chest. The scent of cedar and bergamot captivates my senses. He releases me from the hug and grabs my hand, leads me to his truck, and opens the door for me to get in.

"Of course, you drive this big ass thing." I tease after Choice gets into the driver's seat. "I like it though."

"I'm a big man. I can't drive around in a clown car."

Choice pulls out of my driveway, taking a few turns before he hops on I-96 towards downtown. With it being the wintertime, there are so many places he could be taking us. The ride lasts about fifteen minutes and in those fifteen minutes, we learned quite a bit about each. He's a pediatric nurse, a middle child whereas I am the oldest, he has graced the earth with his presence for 32 years, and his favorite pizza topping is black olives.

"Black olives? Yuck." I say pretending to puke. "Pass me the pineapples."

"Woman, I almost put you out my car. This is a no pineapples zone!"

We laugh a bit before he asks me about my practice as a sex therapist. I gave him a quick explanation that I don't stand around coaching people how to have sex. It's more like breaking through emotional and mental barriers to engaging in sex while assisting them to have a better relationship with their partner.

"I respect you chose a profession that is underrated but necessary. So much could be avoided if we talk to our partners and express our needs." He glances at me across the cab of the truck.

"Thank you. I love my job although it can be stressful which, as a pediatric nurse, I'm sure you can understand. I don't know if I'd be able to handle seeing all those kids so sick."

"It doesn't get easier I can say that. I always rejoice harder for the kids I can help."

We fall into a lighter conversation as we come up on the exit that will lead us toward downtown where rival coney islands sit on the corner. We park on the side of the road and as I'm about to open the door, Choice stops me.

"Remove your hand from the door, Tru. When you are in my presence, there will never be a door you open yourself. Don't touch another handle."

Properly chastised, I snatch my hand away from the door like it burned me. Choice checks his mirror before getting out and coming around to my side of the truck. He opens the door and helps me onto the snowy sidewalk. Closing the door, he grabs my hand, holding it as we stride toward the end of the block. A lit-up Christmas tree comes into view as well as an ice skating rink right in the middle of Campus Martius Park.

I glance at him, then to the rink. "Um, Choice?"

"Yes, gorgeous?" He answers.

"Are we going ice skating?"

"Yes. Is that okay?" Choice stops us and turns me towards him. "I figured we could do something that forced us to laugh and have fun. I'm not a pro at ice skating but I figured I could endure some jokes at my expense if I fall and bust my ass."

I giggled. "I've never been ice skating so this will be something fun for us both."

I pull him with me towards the tent to get our skates. We stand in line a few minutes before the attendant hands

7

us the skates and we shuffle our way to the seats provided to strap up and get on the ice.

My first step on the ice is smooth but each one after had me clinging to Choice like my life depended on it. He's tried to coax me into taking a few more steps but I am not having it. He switched places with me but that only ended with the both of us falling flat on our asses and laughing so hard that the skating rink attendant had to come over and help us, which led to the attendant also falling.

I had to give it to Choice. This is shaping up to be the best date ever.

CHAPTER THREE

Choice

WE SKATE around the rink a few more times before the chill started to get to Tru. I lead her to the opening of the rink, and we shuffle our way over to the tent that houses the hot chocolate stand.

We step into the tent and the heat in here is on full blast. It's warm but the initial chill is still lingering on my skin. Tru is shivering like she's been stuck outside in a blizzard, which I guess she has seeing as it's 20 degrees out there. I lead her over to one of the heat lamps, sitting her right next to it.

"I'm gonna get you some hot chocolate to help warm you up," I tell her before walking over to the concession stand and ordering us both a large hot chocolate. I peek over my shoulder to glance at the brown-skinned beauty I came with. Tru is huddled into herself, trying to preserve all the body heat she can. The tip of her nose and her cheeks are red from the bite of cold whipping past us as we skated. Her thick thighs shake from the bouncing of her feet to keep her lower half warm.

Gathering my order, I make my way to her.

"I-I'm shaking like a cold s-stripper out here." Tru chatters between shivers.

"We'll get you warmed up in no time. Here, drink this." I laugh at her statement and hand her the Styrofoam cup. She blows on it before taking a sip. She releases a moan, rocking in her seat, and my body reacts by rushing blood south. God, if I could hear nothing else but that for the next millennium, I would be a happy man. Tru maintains eye contact with me and licks her lips.

Oh, so that's the game she wants to play.

"Sheesh. My hands are still cold." Tru says rubbing them together.

Putting down my drink, I grab her hands, remove both of our gloves and rub her hands between mine to help generate a little warmth. I run warm so it's the least I can do to help her stop shivering. I place her hands near my mouth, blowing on them to help warm them a bit more. I kiss her fingers and the back of her hands.

"Tell me something else about you." I inquire to get her mind off her frozen fingers. I continue rubbing her hands between mine, dropping small kisses on every piece of skin affected by the cold.

"What do you want to know?"

I pause, before continuing my previous actions. "What's your favorite comfort food?"

"My favorite is apples with chocolate hazelnut spread. I can literally eat that combo all day." Tru's eyes are on me as I continue kissing her hands.

"What other things do you like? What's your favorite TV show?" I ask.

"Um..." she pauses, her breathing increasing. "I don't watch much TV. I am more likely to read a book."

"Tell me about your favorite book," I ask, placing kisses on her wrists.

"I, um..." Tru starts.

"You, um?" I prompt her knowing she has lost a bit of focus. "Finish what you were saying, Tru. I'm listening."

"I can't concentrate when you do that." She doesn't remove her hands from my grip.

I place the tip of her finger in my mouth, sucking lightly. Tru's sharp intake of breath has me looking into her pretty brown eyes.

"Choice, please stop before I lose my manners." She says lowly, eyes bright with her desires.

I lean forward, getting into her space, staring into her eyes. Her pupils are blown wide, almost eclipsing her irises. She doesn't move backward and doesn't drop her gaze in a show of courage. I like that about her and plan to use it to her advantage.

I'm a breath away from our lips touching for the first time when I say, "Then lose them."

Tru leans forward, pushing our lips together. She lets out a low moan as our lips and tongues tangle together. The kiss is all-consuming and tells me there is nothing shy about this woman. Tru knows what she wants and goes straight for it, plowing ahead until it's in her grasp. Her lips are pillow soft and taste the hot chocolate she's consumed.

She runs her hands up my chest until they land on my cheeks, cupping my face to keep me right where she wants me. I lick every corner of her mouth to taste all of her. I'm glad I'm sitting because a kiss like this would drive me to my knees, ready to give Tru any and everything she asked for.

The sounds of the tent flap opening bring us to reality, and we break the kiss. Staring into her eyes, unbridled lust and desire look at me. If there weren't people around, I'm pretty sure Tru would climb in my lap.

Leaning my forehead against hers, I close my eyes and breathe her in. "Finish your hot chocolate. I need you to warm up a little more before we go outside."

She sits back in her chair keeping her eyes locked on mine. I would give anything to read her mind right now with the way she is rubbing her thighs together and clenching her hands. I'd say I'm pretty sure I know what she wants. Lucky for her, I'm happy to provide it to her in droves.

We finish our drinks in silence. Looks exchanged between us are full of the craving we have for one another.

"What do you need, Tru?" I ask her.

She takes a moment to answer. Thinking it over in her mind before giving me an answer I'm pretty sure I already know. Leaning forward, she says, "I want you to take me home and fuck me six ways from Sunday."

I widen my eyes a bit, taken off guard by her response, before giving her a slight nod. I gather our trash in one hand and Tru in the other before leading us to the tent to drop off our skates. While expecting her to ask me to take her home, I didn't expect her to tell me like that. Women who are aggressive in asking men for what they want are my weakness.

I love that tough shit.

CHAPTER FOUR

Choice

I GET Tru in the car in record time before heading towards my home in Rosedale Park. I'm sure I broke a couple traffic laws to get home in under fifteen minutes but, you do what you must when a woman is asking you to fuck her the way Tru has. I'm gonna give her everything she asked of me and more. If she's not trying to hide in my bushes, playing nineties RnB through a speaker once we are done, I didn't do my job.

I pull my truck into the driveway and as I turn the car off, out of the corner of my eye, I see Tru reaching for that fucking door handle. She must think I'm playing with her ass. I grab her by the arm, gently pushing her back in her seat, and sliding my hand around her neck, squeezing softly. A devilish grin glides across her face and her eyes twinkle with mischief. That small smile has me thinking I am gonna have to work her lil' vexatious ass out. I bring her face close to mine, mingling our breath together.

"What I tell your ass about touching doors in my presence?" I scold.

Just like the brat she is, Tru whispers, "I heard what you said. I decided not to listen."

I flash her a smile. "That's okay. You'll learn that lesson before the night is over. You can bet that."

I get out of the car and thankfully, Tru waits for me to open the door like I asked of her. I extend my hand to her to help her onto the ice and slush. Careful to keep her from slipping, I grip her hand as I usher her to my front door. Unlocking the heavy wooden door, I push it open to allow Tru to enter first. She knocks snow and slush off the bottom of her shoes before stepping through. I step through the threshold, giving my boots the same treatment before turning to close and lock the door behind me.

Returning my attention to Tru, I realize she has moved closer to me, allowing me to smell the perfume she wore on our date. The warm vanilla and creamy sandalwood pull me deeper into her orbit. Before I can blink, Tru wraps her arms around my neck. Kissing my lips, down to my neck, and up to my ear before biting my earlobe. She dips her tongue in my ear and my body releases a full shiver.

"You cold or something?" Tru teases, raining small kisses from my temple to my chin.

"Nah. I've never had anybody to lick my ear like that. Didn't expect to like that shit."

She smirks as she continues her journey to explore more of my body. She grips the zipper of my coat, exposing the shirt I have on underneath it. Tru pushes at my coat as it slides down my arms. I reach behind me to hang it up before removing Tru from the warm outer layers she still has on.

I step away from Tru, blocking her attempts to undress me. I need to see her, all of her before I can allow myself the gift of her skin against mine. Her dark blue sweater accentuates the golden tones in her skin while her jeans make her look like she had been poured into them. If she looks this good in clothes, I'm gonna have a hard time seeing her without them.

"C'mere." I beckon her to come closer. I need to get her out of these clothes and spread across my bed. If the hardened length pressing behind my jeans is any indication, I need to feel Tru's skin like I need my next breath. The craving to have her under me is pumping in my veins as I start to expose the soft, caramel-colored skin of her belly, lifting her sweater over her head and discarding it who knows where.

Tru's heavy breasts, held up by the sexiest bra I have ever seen, pull at my attention. I rub a thumb over her hardened nipples teasing me through the material. She sucks in a shuddering breath at the sensation. Her skin is flushed with arousal. I won't keep her waiting long. Her body needs to be worshiped the right way and I won't be rushed in doing my due diligence to provide every ounce of pleasure I can.

I undo the button on her jeans, pushing them to her ankles, and prompting her to lift one leg, then the other after removing her boots. Pausing with my face eye level to the black lace covering her pussy, I incline my head towards her center. I breathe in the natural scent from between her legs as if it's the ambrosia of the deities. I want to run my tongue through her folds, sampling her flavor and commit it to memory. Not yet though.

Patience, Choice.

I give my attention to the apex of her thighs and place small kisses across her mound with the last right on her clit. Tru's watching me with keen eyes, and I can't hold back the small smile I give her. I love when her eyes are on me, watching every move. Standing to my full height, I tower over Tru, bringing her gaze upwards. I capture her lips again in a slow, lazy kiss.

Cupping her cheeks, I say, "I hope you know if you let me slide between your legs, you not going nowhere."

Tru doesn't respond. Instead, she slides her hands from

where they sit on my abs towards the waistband of my jeans. Unsnapping the buttons and pulling on the zipper gives her unobstructed access to grip my already hard dick.

"We'll see," she answers, stroking my shaft.

That shit she talking has me riled up. She thinks I'm playing with her fine ass, but I can always show her better than I can tell her.

CHAPTER FIVE

CHOICE's dick throbs in my hand. I haven't seen it yet, but the girth has my pussy clenching around nothing. I tighten my grip around the base of the warm flesh in my hand. Choice leans his head against the door, letting out a groan that rumbles in his chest. He closes his eyes and swipes his tongue across his lips.

"Fuck, that feels good," Choice groans.

I pull the top of his pants down to get a good look at the thick head dripping pre-cum all over my hand. I swipe my thumb over the bead dragging it down his shaft, paying close attention to the soft curve underneath. Choice lets out a hiss, the sound motivates me to continue to stroke him to the edge of his sanity. Over and over I move my hand, waiting to see euphoria fill his body. His hips rock with my hand, increasing the friction he's desperate to chase.

"I'm close," Choice says, swallowing as he falls victim to my ministration. "Slow up for me. I'm not ready to nut."

I ignore him and keep moving my wrists. My desire to see him come undone is too strong for me to stop.

"Tru, baby girl," Choice pleads. "Hold on."

I must drift too close to the sun because his hand shoots out to grip my hand and put an end to the game I'm playing with him. Choice lifts his head, locking eyes with me. All playfulness from earlier is gone. His gaze has turned predatory, and I would be lying if I said I wasn't excited at the prospect of my soul getting snatched from the back of my pussy.

Leaning close to me, Choice's breath washes over my face. His brown eyes hold every ounce of wanting to break through.

"Any time I nut will be inside you. Whether it be your pretty ass mouth or what I know will be that tight lil' pussy between your legs."

Fingers slide up my neck before Choice grips me by the roots of my braids causing me to release a gasp. His lips crash onto mine. The kiss is hungry, desperate. Our teeth clash while our mouths slide against one another. Every whimper, every small sound, Choice swallows it and provides one of his own. Men don't often make noise during sex and I, for one, go feral for a man comfortable enough with himself to show his pleasure vocally.

Without warning, I am in the air. My legs wrap around Choice's waist to hold on for dear life. I dip my head to nip at his collarbone and shoulder. Choice takes steps away from the front door, kicking his shoes off in the process of taking us deeper into his home. I wish I had the time to appreciate it, but I will have to settle for knowing his home smells like him. Warm laundry, fresh wood, citrus, and a hint of leather.

We enter a bedroom and without putting me down, he reaches over and turns on the bedside lamp. The light emitting from it is enough to see but dark enough to keep the mood sensual and intimate. Choice approaches the king-sized bed and sets me on it. He pushes on my shoulder, signaling he wants me to lay back.

Hovering over me, Choice continues our make-out session. He brings a hand to palm my breast before rolling it across my nipples, eliciting a moan to bubble from my throat.

In between kisses against the skin of my neck, Choice mutters, "I'm going to take care of you in all the ways you crave. Would you like that?"

I nod my head because words have escaped me.

"Words, Tru."

"Y-yes. I would like that."

Choice lifts his body from mine, and I reach to pull him to me. He chuckles, evading my reach, before bending to reach behind me. He removes my bra, placing kisses on the top of each breast. Continuing downward, he sucks my nipples into his mouth. Choice moves his tongue across the nub before biting slightly. The sharp sting is soothed away by another wet swipe of his tongue. Choice pays equal attention to each breast, refusing to let one be left out too long.

I'm gyrating my hips against his thigh to apply pressure on the bundle of nerves screaming at me for release. I won't have to wait long as I watch Choice kiss his way down my body. He slips his fingers into the seat of my panties as he comes eye to eye with the treasure situated between my legs. Pulling the fabric to the side, Choice's eyes flick to mine before returning to my pussy glistening with my arousal.

He slides a finger through my slit, and I groan at the contact. Lifting his hand to his mouth, Choice samples my nectar. His eyes slide close, opening when my juices have been wiped clean from his finger.

"You taste good as fuck," Choice's deep voice utters.

He dips into my slit, coating his fingers in my arousal, and rubbing his wet fingers against each exposed nipple. The air breezing past my wet nipples makes me shiver. The chill is replaced by Choice's warm mouth. The sensations overtake my senses and I find myself on the edge as if I am about to climax.

"This pussy too good to let another nigga get a taste. I'm putting a claim on this shit."

Choice pulls me to the edge of the bed, resting my ass on the end. Pulling my panties to the side, he leans in to drag his tongue against the wetness of my pussy.

"Choice." I moan, unable to hold onto the rush of pleasure.

His tentative tasting turned into a full-out feast. A growl of frustration rips from him with my panties being in the way of his meal. He slides his thumbs into my waist-band, pulling them towards my thighs. I lift my hips to assist him in their removal and as soon as they are gone, he dives in.

Choice alternates between sucking my clit and giving me broad strokes with his tongue. All of this is driving me fucking crazy. My body tingling from the impending orgasm that has me standing on the edge of a cliff. I tense as I prepare for the full body release Choice's tongue is plunging me towards. It's so close I can taste it.

"I'm so close. Please. Please, " I moan out.

Choice tongue increases in speed, flickering over my bundle of nerves, nibbling my sensitive flesh, and as I am about to fall into orgasmic bliss, he stops. My well-deserved orgasm dissipates and my eyes snap open to Choice's smug grin and wet face.

"Choice, please," I beg.

"Please what?" The asshole blinks at me in faux inno-cence. He places his hand on my pussy, taunting me with the tips of his fingers at my entrance.

"Make me cum." I say, winding my hips to help rebuild the orgasm he refuses to give me.

"You know, I like you like this, begging and pleading." Choice's eyes are locked on my lower body, watching the circling path his fingers are on. His warm breath washes over my lower set of lips and it sets off a small tremble in my body.

Choice's fingers find their way into my canal. He curls his fingers and finds my G-Spot. If that wasn't enough, he sucks my clit into his mouth with a vengeance. I cup my breast, pulling at my sensitive nipples adding to the already overwhelming sensations I'm experiencing.

I'm so close to cumming, I can taste it.

I'm right there.

Almost.

There.

The telltale signs are there and then nothing. Choice stops the delicious movement of his fingers against my vaginal walls and lets the orgasm die off before starting his torturous cycle again. Massaging the rough ridges of my g-spot, leading me right to the cusp of orgasm before slowing to a crawl. Enough friction to keep me going but not enough to push me over. I'm damn near in tears from the constant edging.

"Choice," I plead. Lifting my head and locking eyes with him, I continue. "If I don't cum, I promise I will die. I will do whatever you want, anything you need. Please. Let me have it. I won't ask for nothing else. Please. Just le-"

My tirade is cut off because Choice flicks out the tip of his tongue to lick my sensitive clit and I detonated; words left on the tip of my tongue choking me. I arch away from the mattress as wave after wave splash over my body, putting me in a height of bliss I never knew existed. Stars burst behind my shut eyelids as I drift to Earth.

I open my eyes looking at Choice before closing them

again. He is still laying on his stomach looking at me with wonder and amazement in his eyes. After the orgasm I had from his dangerous ass lips and tongue, I need to be careful with his ass.

CHAPTER SIX

Choice

EXPERIENCING Tru succumbing to orgasm is better than anything I could imagine. The way she squeezes her eyes closed, the scrunch of her nose, the way she bites her lower lip trying to keep the screams inside. It's beautiful.

That small glimpse into her climax has turned me ravenous, nothing short of possessive of any pleasure her body receives. I slide up the bed and position my body over Tru to watch her come back to herself.

Tru's big, brown eyes open, connecting with mine. Her gaze darts about my face, looking for something and she must find it because she pulls me closer to her. Propping herself on her elbows, she kisses me with more passion than I expected. Her tongue darts out to slide across my lips and she groans at the combined taste of us. My beard and lips are still covered in her essence, wet from the time I took between her thighs.

"Fuck you are so pretty," I rub her cheek with my thumb. "I could stare at you all day."

She scoffs and shakes her head as her pretty brown skin turns a bit pink. I frown a bit wondering why she doesn't believe me. I shelf that to ask her about later because my need to feel all of her biblically is too strong.

I stand to discard the rest of my clothes. Tru's eyes are on me the entire time. With each item I remove, Tru presses her thighs together and her breath intake speeds up, panting through the lust-filled haze she's tangled in. Standing before her, naked as the day I was born while stroking myself, I take in Tru's body admiring everything the good Lord saw fit to bless her with.

The stretch marks adorning her thighs, travel to the small amount of pudge in her belly pronounced by the curves of her waist and the expansion of her hips. I want to trace each line, her skin like velvet under my fingertips. Tru's breasts are decorated with dark brown nipples begging for more of my attention. A small tattoo of an arrow on her right bicep peeks out at me. This woman is breathtaking and if I do nothing else, I will make sure she knows it. Tru's arms start to rise, and she goes to cover herself.

Oh, fuck no.

"Move your arms out my way, Tru," When she clears my view, I continue. "Don't hide shit from me. I'm admiring your body and how well you tend to her. I'm not staring for no other reason besides you are gorgeous as fuck and I wonder what I did right to get a chance to be in your atmosphere. I'm staring because I'm so enamored with how you look I want to commit every detail to memory." To add a point to my statement, my dick jumps. Her eyes flick from my throbbing shaft to my eyes. She licks her lips and repositions herself, so she is on her hands and knees facing me.

Tru crawls across the bed stopping before the end of the bed. She grips my dick again, stroking me. My eyes roll to the back of my head before I settle my vision on her once more.

"I want you to fuck my face," she tells me. I would be less of a man to deny her anything she wants right now.

"Open ya mouth then pretty girl," I tell her. I move Tru's hand, replacing it with my own. I rub the tip across her bottom lip before pushing myself inside her warm, waiting mouth. I start to move into her. The large vein at the underside of my erection slides across her tongue as I hit the back of her throat. Tru gags a little and the action tightens her throat around me. I groan out at the brief spasm, rolling my head around my shoulders, but I continue fucking her mouth like she asked.

The sound of Tru swallowing my dick whole fills the room. A primal need to mark her throat with my seed comes over me and I speed up my thrusts. I treat her mouth like I'm going to treat her pussy, with a twisted sense of reverence. The wet suction pulls me deeper into her throat until Tru's nose bumps against my pelvis with each thrust.

Spit drips from her chin and my balls, splattering against her thighs and chest. She pauses her mission of sucking my dick to take my balls into her mouth. One at a time, she shows them attention and amplifies my need to bust all over her face. Once she has shown them enough attention, Tru deep throats my dick again, bobbing her head to a pace she's comfortable with.

One of Tru's hands disappears before the other is removed from sight, too. I realize the location when there's a slight tugging on my balls and I see her playing with her clit. Witnessing her take her own pleasure and mine, brings the beginning of my climax out of nowhere.

"You gonna swallow my cum?" I ask her, still delivering punishing thrusts into her mouth. Tru nods her head as much as she can with her mouth still so full of my dick. Her eyes locked on mine. Both of us refused to be the first to look away.

"Good girl. You better not waste a drop either." A loud moan reverberates from her throat and I'm a goner. My balls contract and I erupt onto her tongue, forcing her to swallow around me.

I thrust a final time, releasing the rest of the tension built up before pulling out of her mouth. Tru, deciding we weren't done yet, flicks out her tongue, gathering the bead of cum left on my tip. Fuck, she's so beautiful when she's being nasty as fuck. Tru opens her mouth showing me all she sucked from me. A curse falls from my lips as a drop of my cum rolls out from the side of her mouth. I wipe it up with my thumb before pushing my thumb, and what she spilled, into her mouth forcing her to swallow.

I'm panting, unable to gather myself and slow my breath.

"You are a goddamn demon, you know that? There's no way you need to be out here sucking anybody up like that. I promise I'm going to jail behind that head if you give it to other niggas."

"Then take me off the market, Choice. I'm free to do what I want if I'm single."

While she has a point, I'm not trying to hear that. " Yeah, okay. I got something for that ass."

CHAPTER SEVEN

"I GOT SOMETHING FOR THAT ASS."

That's the last thing I hear before Choice somehow grabs me by the ankle and yanks me to the end of the bed, connecting the back of my thighs and his pelvis. His strong hands move from my calves to grip me behind the knees, spreading them apart. My glistening center is open to his gaze.

Choice hovers over my pussy. I lean my head to the side to get a look at what he's doing, and he looks right at me. He gets a glint in his eye and slides his wide tongue against my lower lips. I hiss out a breath, lifting my hips to keep his tongue right where I need it. Choice moves out of reach, and I pout from being denied.

He smirks at me knowing what he did and what I wanted. Repositioning himself to kneel on the bed, his skin is warm against my own as his dick presses against the inside of my thigh. Choice moves his hips, aligning his massive erection with my honey pot, sliding himself against me. A small squelching sound echoes through the air as we slide against each other. The tip of him making brief contact with my clit before backing away.

I don't know what it is about him wanting to tease and edge me but, I've had enough. I reach between us and grip him in my fist.

I need him inside me. He surrounds me, stretching me open to receive every inch. I get him inside my entrance and my eyes drift close, overwhelmed by the amount of stimulation I'm already receiving with the tip in. I move my hand out of the way trusting Choice will continue the pleasure I'm desperate to receive.

"Open your eyes Tru," Choice demands. "I need you to watch me stroke this fat ass pussy."

I shudder at the command and follow it without delay. With my eyes wide open, I watch Choice thrust into my body. His face frowns up and the music of our connection flows through the air.

His eyes lock with mine and I am filled with a secondary emotion that runs as strong as the lustful feelings boiling over. I've met a kindred spirit. Someone that gets me and the connection we have is stronger than anything else I have experienced. I have known this man all of 24 hours and I'm falling for him.

Choice changes his stroke from slow and deep to hitting angles that have me ready to climb walls. His arms wrap around my waist, holding me in place with his weight.

"I know you not fuckin' runnin' from this dick," he growls. Choice starts to stroke me deeper, causing my body to tense. "Why you wanna play with me, huh? This what you wanted, so stop tryna take my pussy from me."

I'm out of my mind, swimming through seas of sexual bliss when I roll over into my second orgasm. I scream my way through it before dissolving into gasps as his stroke never falters through the death grip my pussy has on him.

Looking at me, he says "I'ma treat you like a princess

out in public, but inside these walls, I'ma fuck you like a slut. You good with that?"

I could do nothing but nod my head as words escaped me yet again. I couldn't form words to save my life right now. He's delivering death strokes, making me take every bit of power and strength he gave behind each one.

Choice must have noticed my dilemma and slowed his pace a bit. Keeping his weight pressed on me, he lays his forehead on my shoulder while giving me kisses on my shoulder and collarbone, pecking my lips a few times, before landing on the side of my head to whisper in my ear. He tells me I'm beautiful. Giving me words of affirmation to solidify what he thought of me and what I oughta be thinking about myself.

"I can't help but want to lift you up. Make you feel good about yourself regardless of what other niggas may have put in your head. I'm on a mission to rearrange all that shit so you believe you are the Queen around this bitch. You should accept and act as nothing less. You will stand on your own ground and command respect from me and anybody else in your path because you deserve it."

Lord, tell this man to hush!

This man has the kind of dick that makes me throw caution to the wind and beg him to fill me with his baby. The kind that would have me popping up to his job unannounced, being clingy, and pouting when he needs to leave the room for a second to relieve himself. To pair this kind of man to the words of affirmation falling from his lips, I don't know what I did to get myself into this but I sure as fuck refuse to get myself out of it.

"I'm gonna cum. Please Choice. I'm right there, baby. Put your stamp on this pussy. Oh, fuck!" I scream.

"Let that shit go, ma. Soak my shit."

I whimper as I explode into a million tiny pieces. My mind fragmented as I fall off the edge into the strongest orgasm I have ever had. With the strength of my orgasm, I'm still juicing around him. His stroke is assisted by the wetness I provided him, and he is putting it to good use.

"I'm gonna nut all in my pussy. That's what you want, Tru?"

"Yes," I gasp out. "Please."

"Fuck, this wet ass pussy," Choice grunts, speeding up his strokes to chase his orgasm. "Come for me again, Tru. I need one more, pretty girl."

It's like my pussy lives to please him because I cum again almost on command. Choice fucks me through this orgasm before following behind me. His face is the picture of bliss as he falls into euphoria. After he releases the last of his orgasm into my womb, we lay together, exhausted, tired, and well fucked.

"You sure you meant what you said about me being yours?" I ask him in a small voice. I can handle rejection but his words of assurance to me unlocked a desire I didn't know I had.

"I meant every word." Choice rumbles, accentuating his statement with a kiss to my temple.

Choice slides us under his thick blanket, settling my head on his fluffy pillows. Choice spoons himself behind me, pulling me flush against his chest. My eyes drift close as my breathing evens out.

"Rest up, baby girl. I got another round in me."

EPILOGUE

THREE YEARS LATER...

"Raspberry Leaf Tea!"

The barista is slinging orders left and right today. I came to people-watch and sip on my non-caffeinated beverage. I had to change my order for a little while. Lord knows I miss my lattes. I go to stand, and a hand shoots out to rest on my arm. My eyes find my husband's brown eyes staring at me in disapproval.

"Sit your ass down, Tru. I'm not gonna keep chasing you around when you know the doctor told you to stay off your feet. I'll get your weird ass tea," Choice grumbles after standing from the corner table I snagged when we got here.

"Okay, okay. Just make sure that they put-"

"Lemonade, not water, with an extra scoop of ice, add a pump of classic syrup with a bagel and cream cheese on the side. I know your order like the back of my hand, pretty girl. I got this." He kisses my cheek and goes to get my order.

Choice is still as bossy as the first time we met. He refuses to let me lift a finger ever since we learned I became pregnant. I'm ready to pop any day now with our baby boy.

We got married about six months after our first date. We couldn't spend much time without each other, knowing that we became each other's soulmates. It made sense to take our relationship to the point we made it legal. We had a small ceremony with our friends and family at the observatory on Belle Isle. Choice decided he didn't wanna spare any expense and decorated the entire place with the finest of everything, including my dress that had been made by a well-known designer.

Spending time with and loving Choice is easy. He made it easy. There wasn't an argument or disagreement that he wasn't patient with. He sat with me, listening to me rant, and then when it is his turn he spoke calmly to me, voicing his opinion or disagreements. His demeanor when it came to me always reminded me I deserved a fierce kind of love that is patient and kind, especially during trying times. Choice will rub my feet, speak positivity into me, and fuck me sideways when the time called for it. While it's no wonder this little bun in the oven popped up, I'm surprised it popped up this late.

"He loves the hell out of you, I swear." A voice sounds from my left.

I give my attention to Theory, Choice's brother who lives in Houston. He came to visit for a few weeks needing a break from the city. He's the reason I know about raspberry leaf tea in the first place. The man knows so much about herbs and plants.

I roll my eyes. "And I love his big head ass when he not being Mr. Bossy. I can walk 15ft to the damn counter."

Theory laughs loudly, disturbing the table next to us. "You know damn well that man would have turned this coffee shop on its head if you would have hurt yourself walking to that counter."

I huff at him knowing he's right. Choice is so protective over me and this pregnancy. If I stub my toe, he'd be fussing over me for the next two weeks. I keep reminding him I'm pregnant, not disabled but, it does no good since it goes in one ear and right out the other.

Choice grabs my drink and brings it to me, sitting it next to my bagel before I dive right in.

"Damn, Tru. Is it you or the baby that's hungry?" Theory asks. Choice punches him on the arm, scowling at him.

"Apologize before she cries, and I have to call momma to plan a funeral."

"I'm sorry you are stuck with this dick head for the rest of your life." Theory mutters.

"The two of y'all are a mess. Anyway Theory, when are you going back to Houston, and when am I invited to your herbal shop?"

"Y'all can come whenever. I need your help anyway, Tru. I'm trying to entice the woman I saw a few weeks ago to go on a date with me but she's paying me dust right now. In my spirit, she's the one for me. I know it."

"She probably thinks you one of them mouth-breathing, creepy niggas." Choice jokes.

"Nah, man. This one is serious. I want her on my arm, in my bed, and on my life insurance. The relationship the two of y'all have inspired me to hang up my player ways and settle down." Theory says looking at the table.

I place my hand on his shoulder and my other hand on Choice's thigh. "She'll come around. Be patient with her."

Choice kisses my hand and urges me to drink my tea so he can take me home and rub my swollen ankles.

This man loves me so deeply another man couldn't dream of making me feel the way he does. I got the once-in-a-lifetime chance to love him because of our love for coffee and really, I wouldn't have it any other way.

THE END

PLAYLIST

Check Out the Songs I listened to while writing
Coffee Break

https://tinyurl.com/4hjytysu

ACKNOWLEDGMENTS

So, to start off this long list of people to thank, I have to thank my Mom, Melba, for being my cheerleader through my harebrained ideas. You didn't get to read this book when it was released but I know you'd love it just because I wrote it. This book helped me to mourn you in the best way I knew how; using the mind that you encouraged me to use no matter what.

To all of my siblings, thank you for holding me together when shit got hard. Thank you for encouraging me to try new things and to branch out. You 10 amazing individuals and all my nieces and nephews are my heart and soul (I would name you all but I don't want my readers to have to read an extra novella). I love you today, tomorrow, and yesterday.

To OJ, thanks for the real life example of Choice snatching Tru across the bed and for listening to my plots when I started writing this "hardcore word porn".

Anaiya, words cannot express the love I have for you. The support you have given me over the years is more than appreciated. Thank you for being my person.

MY ARC READERS AND REVIEWERS! I could kiss you all! Every good and bad review warmed my heart. It gave me what you guys love and didn't love so much to help me improve my writing. I can't wait to take the next ride with you.

To me…. You fucking did that. The cover design, the words, the planning… You fucking did that, and I am So. Fucking. Proud. Of you.

ALSO BY NAVY WINTERS

Big City Romance Series

Coffee Break

Tea Time - Coming August 2023

Whiskey Sour - Coming Late 2023

Red Wine - Coming Late 2023

ABOUT THE AUTHOR

navy
winters

EROTIC ROMANCE AUTHOR

I write stories that make me feel good. Stories
that speak to that little girl from the Westside of
Detroit letting her know that her imagination will
take her far if she just lets it.

The stories I write are for the girls that want to
just live freely in their sexuality, in their
humanity, and to be free in who they are naturally.
It took me a long time to love who I am the way
God made me. Who am I to not encourage others
to do the same?

These stories are of my own heart, my own
fantasies, created to bring a few folks along for
the ride.

Printed in the USA
CPSIA information can be obtained
at www.ICGtesting.com
LVHW070539040823
754034LV00019B/707

9 781922 936363